ca's Leaders

# THE
# *Secretary of*
# STATE

by Lois F. Lewis

BLACKBIRCH®
PRESS

San Diego • Detroit • New York • San Francisco • Cleveland • New Haven, Conn. • Waterville, Maine • London • Munich

Photo credits: cover, back cover, pages 3, 4, 5, 6, 9, 10, 12, 16, 17, 18, 20, 22, 26, 28-29, 30-31, 32 © Creatas; Jefferson, Albright, and Power cover inset, pages 4, 5, 7, 8, 9, 12, 13, 14, 15, 16, 17, 19, 20, 21, 23, 25, 26, 27, 28, 29 © CORBIS; Statue of Liberty cover inset © PhotoDisc; pages 22, 28, 29 © Dover Publications

**LIBRARY OF CONGRESS CATALOGING-IN-PUBLICATION DATA**

Lewis, Lois F.
  The Secretary of State / by Lois F. Lewis.
     p. cm. — (America's leaders series)
  Includes index.
  Summary: An introduction to the Cabinet-level post of Secretary of State, discussing the selection of the Secretary, duties, organizational structure, as well as a sample day's responsibilities.
   ISBN 1-56711-665-5 (hbk. : alk. paper)
  1. United States. Dept. of State—Juvenile literature. 2. United States—Foreign relations administration—Juvenile literature. [1. United States. Dept. of State.] I. Title. II. Series.
  JZ1480 .A4 2003
  327.73—dc21
                                            2002004579

# Table of Contents

## The First Cabinet Position

More than 200 years ago, a group of men wrote a document, the U.S. Constitution, which established the American government. The authors of the Constitution divided the government into 3 separate branches, the legislative branch, the judicial branch, and the executive branch. Under the Constitution, the leader of the executive branch was the president.

Ever since George Washington, the first president, took office, presidents have needed people to help them operate the executive branch. In 1789, the U.S. Congress voted to establish several departments in the executive branch to assist the president. The leader of each department was called a secretary. Together the secretaries formed a group known as the president's cabinet.

*Thomas Jefferson (second from right) was the first secretary of state in the first cabinet under George Washington.*

*Secretary of State Madeleine Albright advises President Bill Clinton during a meeting of foreign leaders.*

The first department created by Congress was the Department of Foreign Affairs. This was formed to help the president handle relations with other countries. Congress also created the position of secretary of state to lead this department. In September 1789, Congress changed the name of the Department of Foreign Affairs to the Department of State. The secretary of state became the first member of the president's cabinet.

The secretary of state is the highest-ranking member in the president's cabinet. If the president dies or can no longer perform presidential duties, the secretary of state is in line to lead the country after the vice president, the Speaker of the House of Representatives, and the senior member of the majority party in the Senate.

### USA FACT

All members of the president's cabinet are paid the same annual salary. In 2002, each cabinet member earned $161,200.

## A Job with Many Duties

The Constitution states that the president "shall have the power . . . to make treaties . . . and . . . shall appoint Ambassadors." The secretary of state is the person who helps the president do that part of his job. He or she is the president's chief adviser on foreign policy. Foreign policy is the way the United States acts toward other countries.

Part of foreign policy involves protecting the United States and its citizens overseas. In 1947, Congress created a special section of the executive branch called the National Security Council (NSC). The secretary of state is a member of the NSC. The NSC advises the president on national security and foreign policy. The vice president, the secretary of defense, the secretary of the treasury, and the national security adviser are also NSC members.

Another part of the secretary's job involves diplomacy—peaceful relations with other nations. The secretary advises the president on the appointment of diplomats. Diplomats are people, such as ambassadors, who represent the United States in foreign countries. The secretary also reports to the president about relations with government officials from other countries who live and work in the United States.

The secretary of state is the head of the U.S. State Department, which employs thousands of people. It is a position that requires a person with the skills to lead others, solve problems, and communicate.

As a leader, the secretary supervises the people who work in all areas of the State Department and the foreign service, in the United States and abroad. The secretary also represents the U.S. government when he or she travels abroad.

When problems occur between the United States and another country, the secretary of state may work to

*Secretary Madeleine Albright attends a summit of the leaders of South American nations.*

The Great Seal of
the United States

*Secretary of State
Colin Powell
speaks at an
economic
summit
meeting.*

build trust and understanding. The secretary works
to maintain good relationships with most nations.
He or she may work out the details of peace
treaties and agreements with other countries before
submitting them to the president for approval.

The secretary is also responsible for building strong
business relations between
countries. He or she may
help to create special agreements with other nations.

The secretary of state
must understand all the
important relationships
that exist between the

## USA FACT

As the leader of the Department of
State, the secretary of state is the
person who has the power to use
the Great Seal, a symbol of the
United States. The Great Seal is used
to stamp official papers, such as
peace treaties and announcements
from the president.

United States and other nations. He or she must issue reports about these relationships and explain the role of the United States in these relationships. The secretary informs Congress and the American people about issues and changes that affect relations between the United States and other countries.

The secretary of state also communicates to Congress in other ways. Both the Senate and the House of Representatives must review and approve all programs of the State Department. The secretary appears before congressional committees to discuss budget expenses.

## Who Helps the Secretary of State?

More than 5,000 people in the State Department work under the secretary. All these people work to carry out the president's foreign policy. Some of the people work in Washington, D.C. Others work in foreign offices, such as embassies and consulates, that handle U.S. foreign relations.

Many people work daily with the secretary of state. The secretary's chief of staff schedules meetings, makes travel arrangements, and handles other matters. Other employees include a deputy chief of staff, a personal secretary, and several assistants. The deputy secretary helps the secretary carry out duties and serves in place of the secretary when needed.

The executive secretariat is another key position in the office of the secretary of state. The secretariat's duties include coordinating work within the State Department and managing relations with the White House.

Also reporting to the secretary are heads of U.S. bureaus. These people are responsible for relations in specific areas of the world such as Asia, Africa, and Europe. They have titles such as under-secretary and assistant secretary.

### USA Fact

The State Department has employees in more than 250 locations around the world.

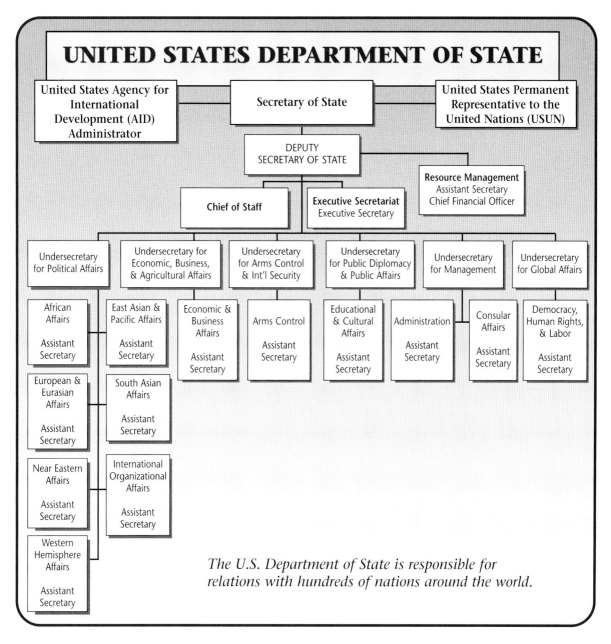

# UNITED STATES DEPARTMENT OF STATE

| United States Agency for International Development (AID) Administrator | Secretary of State | United States Permanent Representative to the United Nations (USUN) |

**DEPUTY SECRETARY OF STATE**

**Resource Management**
Assistant Secretary
Chief Financial Officer

**Chief of Staff**

**Executive Secretariat**
Executive Secretary

| Undersecretary for Political Affairs | Undersecretary for Economic, Business, & Agricultural Affairs | Undersecretary for Arms Control & Int'l Security | Undersecretary for Public Diplomacy & Public Affairs | Undersecretary for Management | Undersecretary for Global Affairs |

- African Affairs — Assistant Secretary
- East Asian & Pacific Affairs — Assistant Secretary
- Economic & Business Affairs — Assistant Secretary
- Arms Control — Assistant Secretary
- Educational & Cultural Affairs — Assistant Secretary
- Administration — Assistant Secretary
- Consular Affairs — Assistant Secretary
- Democracy, Human Rights, & Labor — Assistant Secretary

- European & Eurasian Affairs — Assistant Secretary
- South Asian Affairs — Assistant Secretary

- Near Eastern Affairs — Assistant Secretary
- International Organizational Affairs — Assistant Secretary

- Western Hemisphere Affairs — Assistant Secretary

*The U.S. Department of State is responsible for relations with hundreds of nations around the world.*

The secretary also has authority over the people who operate U.S. embassies in foreign countries. These people are diplomats who have titles such as ambassador, deputy chief of mission, and consular officer.

## Where Does the Secretary Work?

The main office of the secretary of state is located in the U.S. Department of State Building in Washington, D.C. The building is located near the White House.

The secretary works in different areas at the State Department Building. Meetings with leaders from other countries are held in conference rooms. Meetings with department staff workers are held in offices. The secretary speaks to television, newspaper, and magazine reporters in the state department briefing room.

*The State Department Building in Washington, D.C., is located near the White House.*

*Secretary of State Dean Rusk (left) meets privately with President Lyndon Johnson.*

## White House

As a member of the president's cabinet, the secretary attends weekly meetings held in the White House cabinet room. He or she may also meet privately with the president in the Oval Office. The secretary often takes part in special ceremonies, such as meetings, speeches, and dinners, that are held for world leaders at the White House.

## United Nations Headquarters

The United Nations is the world's main international organization for keeping peace. The headquarters of the United Nations is located in New York City.

*The United Nations Plaza in New York City.*

An ambassador who reports to the secretary represents the United States in the United Nations. The secretary may meet at the UN with an ambassador and other representatives, sometimes called delegates, to discuss matters of international importance. The secretary may also make speeches before large groups of world leaders, hold meetings, or attend other events at the UN headquarters.

## American Embassies

The secretary of state often travels to other parts of the world to meet with foreign leaders. When trouble arises in various parts of the world, the secretary may go to the affected regions to see the problem firsthand. He or she will usually meet with leaders to hear their concerns and to offer suggestions for solving the issue.

*The American embassy in Paris, France, sits on land given to the United States by the French government.*

*Indonesian police guard the U.S. embassy in Jakarta, Indonesia, during a time of political unrest.*

When the secretary travels to a foreign country, he or she usually works at the American embassy there. An embassy is a building located in the capital city of a foreign country. The property on which the building sits is given to the United States by the country—just as the United States gives its property to foreign embassies. The embassy staff helps to build relations between the United States and the host country. It also assists Americans who are traveling in that country if problems occur.

## Requirements for Secretary

The Constitution does not give specific requirements for holding an office in the president's cabinet. In many cases, a president will nominate a person for secretary of state who shares his views about foreign policy.

To select a secretary of state, the president looks for a person with strong leadership abilities and experience in foreign relations. Other skills the president might look for include the ability to understand different points of view, patience, and the ability to speak carefully and diplomatically.

*Secretary Madeleine Albright greets U.S. soldiers stationed in Europe.*

*Secretary Colin Powell (left) was a 4-star general in the U.S. Army before he became secretary of state.*

Since 1789, all secretaries of state have been men except one. In 1997, President Bill Clinton nominated Madeleine Albright to serve as secretary of state.

In 2001, President George W. Bush nominated Colin Powell as the first African American to hold the position of secretary of state. Powell had served for 35 years in the U.S. Army and reached the rank of 4-star general. Powell was also the first African American to hold the position of chairman of the Joint Chiefs of Staff, the highest military position in the United States. He was also the national security adviser under President Ronald Regan.

## USA Fact

No members of the president's cabinet can hold an elected office while serving in the cabinet.

## Steps to Approval

Before the president nominates the secretary of state the candidate must undergo a background check—a close review of his or her personal life. The nominee must provide information about finances and other personal matters. Legal experts in the executive branch review the information. They make sure that nothing in the person's background would cause the Senate to reject a nominee or embarrass the president after approval.

Once the background check is completed, the White House announces the nomination publicly. Next, the nominee goes to the Capitol to appear at a hearing of the Senate Foreign Relations Committee. During the hearing, the nominee answers questions from the senators. Often the nominee makes a speech to the committee. The committee then votes on the nomination. If the committee approves, the nomination is sent to all members of the Senate for a vote. If more than half of the senators approve the nomination, the president signs a document that officially confirms the cabinet appointment.

## Swearing-In Ceremony

After the president confirms the cabinet appointment, the appointee is sworn in. This ceremony is often held in the Oval Office at the White House. People who

*President John F. Kennedy announces the nomination of Dean Rusk (left) as secretary of state.*

attend this ceremony include the president, the appointee, members of his or her family, special guests, and members of the news media.

During this ceremony, the appointee takes an oath of office that is very similar to the oath that the president takes during the inauguration ceremony:

*I do solemnly swear (or affirm) that I will faithfully execute the Office of Secretary of State, and will to the best of my ability, preserve, protect and defend the Constitution of the United States.*

The president then gives a statement congratulating the new secretary. The secretary also makes a short speech.

19

## Doing the Job

The responsibilities of the secretary of state have not changed since Thomas Jefferson, the first secretary, took office. Performing the job, however, has changed a great deal. In 1789, the United States was a new nation with relatively little power. Jefferson's State Department had fewer than 20 employees in the United States and abroad. Its budget was slightly more than $50,000 per year.

In the 21st century, the United States is a world superpower. The secretary of state is in charge of more than 5,000 employees in the United States and abroad. The State Department's budget is slightly less than $5 billion per year.

As large as the state department might seem, it is actually smaller than 10 of the 14 cabinet departments.

*Secretary of State James Baker arrives in Kuwait in 1991.*

*Secretary of State George Schultz (second from left) signs an arms control agreement with a representative of the Soviet Union.*

Despite its relatively small size, the department maintains relations with 180 nations and operates more than 250 embassies and consulates.

In order to manage these responsibilities around the world, the secretary of state today is required to spend a great deal of time traveling. That is another change in the job. The first secretary of state to travel on diplomatic business outside of the United States was Elihu Root. In 1906, Root made one trip to South America and visited 7 countries. In 2001, Secretary of State Colin Powell made 12 trips abroad. He visited 37 countries and traveled 148,898 miles!

## A Time of Crisis

When George Washington left office in 1796, cabinet members did not automatically hand in their resignations to the incoming president. The second president, John Adams, kept Washington's cabinet in place. This included Secretary of State Timothy Pickering.

*Timothy Pickering was Washington's fourth secretary of state.*

Adams took office at a time when the United States had signed a treaty with Great Britain and relations were peaceful. On the other hand, France, a U.S. ally in the American Revolution, was engaged in what Adams called a "half war" at sea against the United States. This conflict began in the mid-1790s. It was soon after the people of France revolted against their king and overthrew him in a bloody revolution. The United States was allied with Great Britain—long a foe of France. This made American merchant ships easy targets for the French navy during the first years of the Adams presidency.

In 1798 alone, the French navy seized more than 300 merchant ships. As a result of French actions, many Americans felt that the United States should declare war

*A French warship attacks an American merchant ship in 1798.*

on France. Among those who favored war were Pickering and Alexander Hamilton, the first secretary of the treasury. Adams, on the other hand, knew that sending the new nation to war against one of the most powerful nations in the world would be disastrous.

In the fall of 1799, war fever gripped the United States. Adams held a cabinet meeting. There, Pickering and other cabinet members pleaded with Adams to declare war. Adams resisted the pressure and sent a diplomatic team to France.

Instead of working to assure the success of the diplomatic team, however, the secretary of state undermined Adams. Pickering wrote a series of letters and articles that declared Adams unfit for office.

It so happened that while the American diplomats were traveling to France, General Napoléon Bonaparte took power in France. In late 1799, he signed a treaty that settled all disputes between France and the United States.

Meanwhile, as the election year of 1800 began, the president grew increasingly angry with his secretary of state. He felt that Pickering owed his support to the president he served, not to his personal political views. In May 1800, Adams fired Pickering. It was the first time a president removed a cabinet member from office. From that time on, all cabinet members offered their resignations to an incoming president.

### Another Time of Crisis

Throughout the 1950s and early 1960s, the United States and the Soviet Union were enemies. Each nation possessed nuclear weapons, and this led to a number of tense situations around the world. In 1962, President John F. Kennedy was in office. During that time, the United States discovered that the Soviet Union had placed nuclear missiles in Cuba, just 90 miles from American shores. Kennedy, Secretary of State Dean Rusk, and others in the cabinet were faced with difficult choices. If they allowed the missiles to remain in Cuba, millions of Americans would be in danger of nuclear attack. If the United States attacked the missile sites, however, a nuclear war might occur.

*President John F. Kennedy and Secretary Dean Rusk meet with Soviet representatives to agree on a compromise to end the Cuban missile crisis of 1962.*

At first, Rusk recommended to the president that the United States bomb the missile sites—but only after delivering a warning to Cuba and the Soviet Union. When other cabinet members felt an attack carried too much risk, Rusk suggested a compromise. The United States would agree to remove nuclear missiles that it had placed in Turkey, on the border of the Soviet Union. In return, the Soviets would dismantle the sites in Cuba.

In November 1962, Kennedy ordered the navy to blockade Cuba and prevent Soviet ships from bringing more missiles to the country. He also offered the compromise that Rusk had suggested. After 13 days, the Cuban missile crisis came to an end peacefully.

## A Secretary's Day

The secretary of state works on a busy schedule, attending meetings with world leaders, making speeches, and taking part in other events. Here is what a day might be like for the secretary of state.

6:30 AM   Wake, shower, dress, receive overnight briefings

7:00 AM   Breakfast, read newspaper, prepare for morning news interview

7:30 AM   Morning TV news interview

8:15 AM   Meeting with chief of staff to preview daily schedule

*Secretary Colin Powell (right) attends President George W. Bush's meeting with Mexican president Vicente Fox (left).*

8:45 AM   Meeting with the president of Mexico and press remarks

9:30 AM   Brief meeting with undersecretary for political affairs on border security between the United States and Mexico

*The secretary of state speaks to the press on a daily basis.*

**10:00** AM  Cabinet meeting at White House

**12:30** PM  Host a state department lunch meeting with the president of Mexico and government officials from Mexico

**2:30** PM  Attend meeting with the president of the United States and leaders of foreign affairs from Mexico at the White House

**4:45** PM  Meet with the prime minister of Turkey

**5:00** PM  News radio interview in office

**6:00** PM  Return home; prepare for state dinner

**7:30** PM  Attend state dinner at White House

**10:30** PM  Return home; prepare for trip to China

**11:45** PM  Bed

## Fascinating Facts

**Cordell Hull** served longer than any other secretary of state. Hull was secretary for 11 years under President Franklin D. Roosevelt from 1933 to 1944.

The secretary of state who served the shortest term was **Elihu Washburne**. Washburne served just 11 days before he resigned to become the foreign minister to France.

Six secretaries of state became presidents of the United States. They were **Thomas Jefferson, James Madison, James Monroe, John Quincy Adams, Martin**

*Cordell Hull*

*Thomas Jefferson*

*Elihu Root*

**Van Buren**, and **James Buchanan**. Jefferson also served as vice president under President John Adams.

In the 20th century, 5 secretaries of state were awarded the Nobel Peace Prize. They were **Elihu Root** in 1912, **Frank Kellogg** in 1929, **Cordell Hull** in 1945, **George Marshall** in 1953, and **Henry Kissinger** in 1973.

Over the past 200 years, there have been 65 secretaries of state for the United States. **Daniel Webster** and **James Blaine** served in this office twice.

*Daniel Webster*

# Glossary

**adviser**—a person who provides information and suggestions

**ambassador**—a representative of one country sent to communicate with other countries around the world

**cabinet**—a council of advisers who help manage the government

**Congress**—the legislative branch of government, composed of the Senate and the House of Representatives

**Constitution**—the document that established the U.S. government and that contains the principles and laws of the nation

**diplomacy**—communication between nations

**embassy**—a group of diplomatic ambassadors from one country living in another to represent the interests of their government

**foreign policy**—rules and procedures by which one country interacts with other countries

**Great Seal**—a symbol of the United States, used by the secretary of state to stamp official government papers, such as treaties and presidential announcements

**nominee**—a person who has been proposed to fill a certain position

**United Nations**—an international organization based in New York City responsible for keeping peace and good relations between the nations of the world

## For More Information

### Publications

*American Government.* New York: McGraw-Hill, 2002.

*Holt American Government.* New York: Holt, Rhinehart, and Winston, 2002.

Wellman, Sam and Schlesinger, Arthur M., editor. *The Secretary of State (Your Government: How It Works).* Broomall, PA: Chelsea House Publishers, 2001.

### Web sites

### Department of State archives

http://dosfan.lib.uic.edu/ERC/index.html

A site with comprehensive information on past secretaries of state and the history of the department.

### Secretary of State

http://www.state.gov/secretary

The official secretary of state site, including a daily appointments' schedule, foreign affairs for young people, and "meet the secretary" section.

# Index